THE PERFECT CHRISTMAS

EILEEN SPINELLI

ILLUSTRATED BY
JoANN ADINOLFI

Christy Ottaviano Books
Henry Holt and Company
New York

Henry Holt and Company, LLC
Publishers since 1866
175 Fifth Avenue, New York, New York 10010
mackids.com

Henry Holt® is a registered trademark of Henry Holt and Company, LLC.
Text copyright © 2011 by Eileen Spinelli
Illustrations copyright © 2011 by JoAnn Adinolfi

Library of Congress Cataloging-in-Publication Data
Spinelli, Eileen. The perfect Christmas / by Eileen Spinelli ; illustrated by JoAnn Adinolfi. — 1st ed.
p.   cm.   "Christy Ottaviano Books."
Summary: Two families—one that is perfect and one that is far from it—celebrate Christmas in their own loving ways.
ISBN 978-0-8050-8702-4
[1. Stories in rhyme. 2. Christmas—Fiction. 3. Family life—Fiction.] I. Adinolfi, JoAnn, ill. II. Title.
PZ8.3.S759Pdr 2011   [E]—dc22   2010039213

First Edition—2011 / The artist used gouache, colored pencil, and collage on craft paper to create the illustrations for this book.
Printed in July 2011 in China by Macmillan Production Asia Ltd., Kwun Tong, Kowloon, Hong Kong (Vendor Code WKT).

1 3 5 7 9 10 8 6 4 2

Abigail Archer's family
is perfect as can be.
They drive into the countryside
to chop down their Christmas tree.

Our tree is artificial,
completely out of shape,
with several branches missing
and one held on with tape.

Abigail Archer's mother
hangs holly in the halls,
lights candles on the mantel,
fills bowls with silver balls.

My mom decorates with things
she finds in bargain bins—
a macaroni reindeer
and dented fruitcake tins.

Abigail Archer's grandma
bakes elegant Christmas treats—
a three-tiered tray of gingerbread
and tarts and other sweets.

My grandma's Christmas cookies
could bounce to Mexico.
One fell from Grandma's cookie pan
and broke my uncle's toe.

Abigail Archer's poodle
eats lamb chops from a mat
that's stitched with "Merry Christmas."
He wears a Santa hat.

Our dogs have horrid manners.
They dig through trash for fun.
They slobber in my snow boots.
They jump on everyone.

On Christmas Eve at Abigail's
her relatives come in cars.
Chauffeur-driven! Glamorous clothes!
They look like movie stars.

My relatives come in pickup trucks.
They clatter up the walk.
They *ho-ho-ho* and *jingle bell*.
They shout instead of talk.

Abigail and her cousins
get gifts like queens and kings—
china tea sets, fancy bikes,
kaleidoscopes, and rings.

We get flannel pj's,
a doll, or teddy bear,
a soccer ball, some candy canes,
and lots of underwear.

Abigail plays the cello
to entertain their guests—
some classic Christmas pieces.
She even takes requests.

My father juggles grapefruit
while I play the kazoo.
Then Aunt Clarissa sings off-key.
That's entertainment too!

Then, suddenly it's snowing.
We can't believe our eyes.
We grab our coats. Head out the door.
Ah . . . what a sweet surprise!

The Archers hurry outside too,
awash in streetlamp glow.
Our families are all together,
laughing and dancing
through the snow.